George Colman

The Jealous Wife

A Comedy, in Three Acts

George Colman

The Jealous Wife
A Comedy, in Three Acts

ISBN/EAN: 9783744778305

Printed in Europe, USA, Canada, Australia, Japan

Cover: Foto ©Andreas Hilbeck / pixelio.de

More available books at **www.hansebooks.com**

THE

JEALOUS WIFE.

𝔄 Comedy,

IN THREE ACTS.

BY

GEORGE COLMAN.

LONDON:
SAMUEL FRENCH,
PUBLISHER,
89, STRAND.

NEW YORK:
SAMUEL FRENCH & SON,
PUBLISHERS,
38, EAST 14TH STREET

Characters.

	Drury Lane, 1761.	Olympic, 1855.	Princess's, 1855.
OAKLY	Mr. Garrick.	Mr. A. Wigan.	Mr. C. Kean.
MAJOR OAKLY	Mr. Yates.	Mr. Emery.	Mr. Cooper.
CHARLES	Mr. Palmer.	Mr. Leslie.	Mr. J. F. Cathcart.
RUSSET	Mr. Burton.	Mr. J. H. White.	Mr. F. Matthews.
SIR HARRY BEAGLE	Mr. King.	Mr. Danvers.	Mr. Harley.
CAPTAIN O'CUTTER	Mr. Moody.		...
LORD TRINKET	Mr. O'Brien.	Mr. ... .ning.	Mr. Walter Lacy.
PARIS	Mr. Blaket.		Mr. H. Saker.
WILLIAM	Mr. Ackman.		...
JOHN	Mr. Castle.		Mr. Collis.
TOM	Mr. Clough.		Mr. Cormack.
SERVANT	Mr. Fox.		...
MRS OAKLY	Mrs. Pritchard.	Mrs. Stirling.	Mrs. C. Kean.
LADY FREELOVE	Mrs. Clive.	Miss Castleton.	Mrs. Winstanley
HARRIET	Miss Pritchard.	Miss Marston.	Miss Heath.
TOILET	Mrs. Johnson.	Miss Bromley.	Miss Clifford.
MAID	Mrs. Simpson.		Miss Collis.

Costumes.

MR. OAKLY.—Black velvet coat trimmed with gold, black satin vest embroidered with gold, black satin breeches, black silk stockings, shoes and buckles; white cravat; ruffles; powdered wig and bag.

MAJOR OAKLY.—Scarlet coat with blue and gold facings, gorget and epaulettes; white kersey vest, white pantaloons, Hessian boots; red silk sash; white enamelled sword belt; sword; powdered wig and bag.

CHARLES OAKLY.—Blue coat with gold embroidery, white embroidered vest, white kersey breeches, white silk stockings, shoes and buckles; powdered wig and bag; dress sword and hat; white cravat and ruffles.

LORD TRINKET.—Plum coloured coat with silver embroidery, amber satin vest, embroidered amber satin breeches, white silk stockings, shoes and buckles; dress sword and hat; powdered wig and bag; white cravat and ruffles.

SIR HARRY BEAGLE.—Green square-cut coat trimmed with gold, embroidered vest, leather breeches, top boots; high-crowned round hat; brown wig; huntsman's velvet cap.

RUSSET.—Green great coat trimmed with gold, and black velvet cape; drab square-cut coat, vest, and breeches; top boots; white cravat; brown George wig; three-cornered hat.

JOHN.—Old fashioned white livery coat with aiguilette, red vest, and breeches, white stockings, shoes and buckles; powdered wig and bag; white cravat.

LADY FREELOVE'S SERVANT.—White livery coat, amber livery vest, white kersey breeches, white stockings, shoes and buckles; powdered wig and bag; white cravat.

MRS. OAKLY.—Rich figured amber silk tuck-up dress and petticoat, trimmed with white lace; white dress wig, powdered. *Second dress*—white lace scarf; small velvet hat.

LADY FREELOVE.—Rich white silk tuck-up dress; petticoat, and robe; white dress wig and powder.

HARRIET.—White muslin tuck-up dress and petticoat; broad blue sash: white powdered dress wig. *Second dress*—white lace scarf; brown round hat.

Explanation of the Stage Directions.

R.	R. C.	C.	L. C.	L.
Right.	Right Centre.	Centre.	Left Centre.	Left.

FACING THE AUDIENCE.

THE JEALOUS WIFE.

ACT I.

SCENE I.—*A Room in Oakly's House.*

Noise heard within, R. U. E.

MRS. O. (*within*) Don't tell me—I know it is so—It's monstrous, and I will not bear it.

OAKLY. (*within*) But, my dear!——

MRS. O. Nay, nay, &c. (*squabbling within, L.*)

Enter MRS. OAKLY, R. U. E. *with a letter, followed by* OAKLY.

MRS. O. (L.) Say what you will, Mr. Oakly, you sall never persuade me but this is some filthy intrigue of yours.

OAKLY. (R.) I can assure you, my love——

MRS. O. Your love! Don't I know your—Tell me, I say, this instant, every circumstance relating to this letter.

OAKLY. How can I tell you, when you will not so much as let me see it.

MRS. O. Look you, Mr. Oakly, this usage is not to be borne. You take a pleasure in abusing my tenderness and soft disposition. To be perpetually running over the whole town, nay, the whole kingdom too, in pursuit of your amours! Did not I discover that you was great with mademoiselle, my own woman? Did not you contract a shameful familiarity with Mrs. Freeman? Did not I detect your intrigue with Lady Wealthy? Was not you——

OAKLY. Oons, madam, you throw me out of all patience! Do I know any body but our common friends? Am I visited by any body that does not visit you? Do I ever go out, unless you go with me? And am I not as constantly by your side as if I was tied to your apron strings?

Mrs. O. Go, go, you are a false man. Have not I found you out a thousand times? And have not I this moment a letter in my hand which convinces me of your baseness? Let me know the whole affair, or I will——

Oakly. Let you know! Let me know what you would have of me—you stop my letter before it comes to my hands, and then expect that I should know the contents of it!

Mrs. O. Heaven be praised, I stopped it! I suspected some of these doings for some time past! But the letter informs me who she is, and I'll be revenged on her sufficiently. Oh, you base man, you! (*crosses to* R.)

Oakly. I beg, my dear, that you would moderate your passion! Show me the letter, and I'll convince you of my innocence.

Mrs. O. Innocence! Abominable! Innocence! But I am not to be made such a fool—I am convinced of your perfidy, and very sure that——

Oakly. 'Sdeath and fire! your passion hurries you out of your senses. Will you hear me?

Mrs. O. No; you are a base man; and I will not hear you. (*crosses to* L.)

Oakly. Why, then, my dear, since you will neither talk reasonably yourself, nor listen to reason from me, I shall take my leave till you are in a better humour. So, your servant! (*going*)

Mrs. O. Ay, go, you cruel man! Go to your mistresses, and leave your poor wife to her miseries. How unfortunate a woman am I! I could die with vexation. (L., *throwing herself into a chair*)

Oakly. There it is—now dare not I stir a step further. If I offer to go, she is in one of her fits in an instant. Never sure was woman at once of so violent and so delicate a constitution! What shall I say to soothe her? (*aside*) Nay, never make thyself so uneasy, my dear. Come, come, you know I love you.

Mrs. O. I know you hate me; and that your unkindness and barbarity will be the death of me. (*whining*)

Oakly. I love you most passionately—indeed I do. This must be some mistake.

Mrs. O. Oh, I am an unhappy woman! (*weeping*)

OAK. Dry up thy tears, my love, and be comforted; you will find that I am not to blame in this matter. Come, let me see this letter—nay, you shall not deny me. (*takes the letter*)

MRS. O. There, take it; you know the hand, I am sure.

OAKLY. (*reads*) "To Charles Oakly, Esq." Hand! 'Tis a clerk-like hand—a good round text; and was certainly never penned by a fair lady.

MRS. O. Aye, laugh at me, do!

OAKLY. Forgive me, my love; I did not mean to laugh at thee. But what says the letter? (*reads*) "Daughter eloped—you must be privy to it—scandalous—dishonour-able—satisfaction—revenge"—um, um, um—"injured father,—Henry Russet."

MRS. O. (*rising*) Well, sir, you see I have detected you. Tell me this instant where she is concealed.

OAKLY. So, so, so—this hurts me—I'm shocked. (*to himself*)

MRS. O. What, are you confounded with your guilt? Have I caught you at last?

OAKLY. Oh, that wicked Charles! To decoy a young lady from her parents in the country. The profligacy of the young fellows of this age is abominable. (*to himself*)

MRS. O. (*half aside, and musing*) Charles! Let me see. Charles! No—impossible! This is all a trick.

OAKLY. Such an abandoned action! I wish I had never had the care of him.

MRS. O. Mighty fine, Mr. Oakly! Go on, sir—go on; I see what you mean. Your assurance provokes me beyond your very falsehood itself. So you imagine, sir, this flimsy pretence about Charles is to bring you off. But I am prepared for all your low stratagems.

OAKLY. See there now! Was ever anything so pro-voking? To persevere in your ridiculous—For heaven's sake, my dear, don't distract me! When you see my mind thus agitated and uneasy, that a young fellow, whom his dying father, my own brother, committed to my care, should be guilty of such enormous wickedness—I say, when you are a witness of my distress on this occasion, how can you be weak enough and cruel enough to——

MRS. O. Prodigiously well, sir! You do it very well.

Nay, keep it up—carry it on; there's nothing like going through with it. Oh, you artful creature! But, sir, I am not to be so easily satisfied. I do not believe a syllable of all this. Give me the letter! (*snatches the letter, crosses to* L.) You shall sorely repent this vile business, for I am resolved that I will know the bottom of it!   *Exit,* R. U. E.

OAKLY. Provoking woman! Her absurd suspicions interpret everything the wrong way. But this ungracious boy—in how many troubles will he involve his own and his lady's family. I never imagined that he was of such abandoned principles.

Enter MAJOR OAKLY *and* CHARLES, L. U. E

CHARLES. (L.) Good morrow, sir.

MAJOR O. (C.) Good morrow, brother, good morrow. What, you have been at the old work, I find. I heard you—ding, dong! I'faith, she has rung a noble peal in your ears. But how now? Why, sure, you have had a remarkable warm bout on't. You seem more ruffled than usual.

OAKLY. (R.) I am, indeed, brother; thanks to that young gentleman there. Have a care, Charles; you may be brought to a severe account for this—the honour of a family, sir, is no such light matter.

CHARLES. Sir!

MAJOR O. Hey-day! What, has a curtain lecture produced a lecture of morality? What is all this?

OAKLY. To a profligate mind, perhaps, these things may appear agreeable in the beginning; but don't you tremble at the consequences?

CHARLES. I see, sir, that you are displeased with me; but I am quite at a loss to guess at the occasion.

OAKLY. Tell me, sir,—where is Miss Harriet Russet.
        (*crosses to* C.)

CHARLES. Miss Harriet Russet, sir! Explain.

OAKLY. Have not you decoyed her from her father?

CHARLES. I!—Decoyed her—decoyed my Harriet!— I would sooner die than do her the least injury—What can this mean?

OAKLY. I was in hopes, Charles, you had better principles. But there's a letter just come from her father——

CHARLES. A letter!—What letter? Dear sir, give it me. Some intelligence of my Harriet, Major! The letter, sir! Let me but see this letter, and I'll——

OAKLY. Let you see it!—I could hardly get a sight of it myself. Mrs. Oakly has it.

CHARLES. Has she got it? Major, I'll be with you again directly.   (*crosses and exit hastily*, R. U. E.)

MAJOR O. Hey-day! The devil's in the boy! What a fiery set of people! By my truth, I think the whole family is made of nothing but combustibles.

OAKLY. (L.) I like this emotion—it looks well; it may serve too to convince my wife of the folly of her suspicions. Would to heaven I could quiet them for ever.!

MAJOR O. (R.) Why pray now, my dear naughty brother, what heinous offence have you committed this morning? What new cause of suspicion? You have been asking one of the maids to mend your ruffle, I suppose; or have been hanging your head out at the window when a pretty young woman has passed by, or——

OAKLY. How can you trifle with my distresses, Major? Did I not tell you it was about a letter?

MAJOR O. A letter!—hum—a suspicious circumstance to be sure! What, and the seal a true lover's knot now, hey? or a heart transfixed with darts; or possibly the wax bore the industrious impression of a thimble; or perhaps the folds were lovingly connected by a wafer, pricked with a pin, and the direction written in a vile scrawl, and not a word spelt as it should be! Ha, ha, ha!

OAKLY. Pooh, brother—Whatever it was, the letter, you find, was for Charles, not for me. This outrageous jealousy is the devil. (*crosses to* R.)

MAJOR O. (L.) Mere matrimonial blessings and domestic comfort, brother! jealousy is a certain sign of love.

OAKLY. Love! it is this very love that hath made us both so miserable. Her love for me has confined me to my house, like a state prisoner, without the liberty of seeing my friends, or the use of pen, ink, and paper; while my love for her has made such a fool of me, that I have never had the spirit to contradict her.

MAJOR O. Ay, ay, there you've hit it: Mrs. Oakly

would make an excellent wife, if you did but know how
to manage her.

OAKLY. You are a rare fellow indeed to talk of managing
a wife.—A debauched bachelor—a rattle-brained rioting
fellow—who have picked up your common-place notions
of women in taverns and the camp; whose most refined
commerce with the sex has been in order to delude country
girls at your quarters, or to besiege the virtue of abigails,
milliners, or mantua-makers' 'prentices.

MAJOR O. So much the better!—so much the better!
women are all alike in the main, brother, high or low,
married or single, quality or no quality. I have found
them so, from a duchess down to a milkmaid; every
woman is a tyrant at the bottom. But they could never
make a fool of me. No, no! no woman should ever
domineer over me, let her be mistress or wife.

OAKLY. Single men can be no judges in these cases.
They must happen in all families. But when things are
driven to extremities—to see a woman in uneasiness—a
woman one loves to—one's wife—who can withstand it?
You neither speak nor think like a man that has loved
and been married, major. (*goes up* R. *and sits*)

MAJOR O. I wish I could hear a married man speak my
language. I'm a bachelor, it's true; but I am no bad
judge of your case for all that. I know yours and Mrs.
Oakly's disposition to a hair. She is all impetuosity and
fire—a very magazine of touchwood and gunpowder.
You are hot enough too, upon occasion, but then it's over
in an instant. In comes love and conjugal affection, as
you call it; that is mere folly and weakness—and you
draw off your forces, just when you should pursue the
attack, and follow your advantage. Have at her with
spirit, and the day's your own, brother.

OAKLY. Why, what would you have me do?

MAJOR O. Do as you please for one month, whether
she likes it or not; and I'll answer for it, she will con-
sent you shall do as you please all her life after. In
short, do but show yourself a man of spirit, leave off
whining about love and tenderness, and nonsense, and
the business is done, brother.

OAKLY. I believe you are in the right, major! I see

you are in the right. I'll do it—I'll certainly do it—But then it hurts me to the soul, to think what uneasiness I shall give her. The first opening of my design will throw her into fits, and the pursuit of it, perhaps, may be fatal.

MAJOR O. Fits! ha, ha, ha!—I'll engage to cure her of her fits. Nobody understands hysterical cases better than I do; besides, my sister's symptoms are not very dangerous. Did you ever hear of her falling into a fit when you was not by?—Was she ever found in convulsions in her closet?—No, no, these fits, the more care you take of them the more you will increase the distemper; let them alone, and they will wear themselves out, I warrant you.

OAKLY. True, very true—you are certainly in the right —I'll follow your advice. Where do you dine to-day? —I'll order the coach, and go with you.

MAJOR O. O brave! keep up this spirit, and you are made for ever.

OAKLY. You shall see now, major!—Who's there? (*goes up a little* R.)

Enter SERVANT, L. D. U. E.

Order the coach directly. I shall dine out to-day.

SERV. (L.) The coach, sir?—Now, sir?

OAKLY. Ay, now, immediately.

SERV. Now, sir!—the—the—coach, sir?—that is—my mistress—

MAJOR O. (C.) Sirrah! do as you are bid. Bid them put to this instant.

SERV. Yes—yes, sir—yes, sir.   *Exit* L. D.

OAKLY. (R.) Well, where shall we dine?

MAJOR O. (L.) At the St. Alban's, or where you will. This is excellent, if you will but hold it.

OAKLY. I will have my own way, I am determined.

MAJOR O. That's right.

OAKLY. I am steel.

MAJOR O. Bravo!

OAKLY. Adamant.

MAJOR O. Bravissimo!

OAKLY. Just what you'd have me.

MAJOR O. Why that's well said. But will you do it?

OAKLY. I will.

MAJOR O. You won't.

OAKLY. I will. I'll be a fool to her no longer. But harkye, major, my hat and gloves lie in my study : I'll go and steal them out, while she is busy talking with Charles.

MAJOR O. Steal them! for shame! Pr'ythee take them boldly; call for them; make them bring them to you here; and go out with spirit in the face of your whole family.

OAKLY. No, no—you are wrong—let her rave after I am gone, and when I return, you know, I shall exert myself with more propriety, after this open affront to her authority.

MAJOR O. Well, take your own way.

OAKLY. Ay, ay; let me manage it, let me manage it.

Exit, R. U. E.

MAJOR O. Manage it! ay, to be sure, you are a rare manager! It is dangerous they say to meddle between man and wife. I am no great favourite of Mrs. Oakly's already, and in a week's time I expect to have the door shut in my teeth.

Enter CHARLES, R. U. E.

How now, Charles—what news?

CHARLES. (R.) Ruined and undone! She's gone, uncle, my Harriet's lost for ever.

MAJOR O. (L.) Gone off with a man?—I thought so;—they are all alike.

CHARLES. Oh, no; fled to avoid that hateful match with Sir Harry Beagle.

MAJOR O. Faith, a girl of spirit! but whence comes all this intelligence?

CHARLES. In an angry letter from her father. How miserable I am! If I had not offended my Harriet, much offended her, by that foolish riot and drinking at your house in the country, she would certainly at such a time have taken refuge in my arms.

MAJOR O. A very agreeable refuge for a young lady to be sure, and extremely decent!

CHARLES. What a heap of extravagancies was I guilty of!

MAJOR O. Extravagancies with a witness! Ah, you silly young dog, you would ruin yourself with her father, in spite of all I could do. There you sat, as drunk as a lord, telling the old gentleman the whole affair, and swearing you would drive Sir Harry Beagle out of the country, though I kept winking and nodding, pulling you by the sleeve, and kicking your shins under the table in hopes of stopping you, but all to no purpose. What relations or friends has she in town?

CHARLES. Relations! let me see—faith, I have it! If she is in town, ten to one but she is at her aunt's, Lady Freelove's. I'll go thither immediately. (*crosses to* L.)

MAJOR O. (R.) Lady Freelove's! Hold, hold, Charles! Do you know her ladyship?

CHARLES. (L.) Not much; but I'll break through all to get to my Harriet.

MAJOR O. I do know her ladyship.

CHARLES. Well, and what do you know of her?

MAJOR O. O, nothing!—her ladyship is a woman of the world, that's all.

CHARLES. What do you mean?

MAJOR O. That Lady Freelove is an arrant—by-the bye, did not she last summer make formal proposals to Harriet's father from Lord Trinket?

CHARLES. Yes; but they were received with the utmost contempt. The old gentleman it seems hates a lord, and he told her so in plain terms.

MAJOR O. Such an aversion to the nobility may not run in the blood. The girl, I warrant you, has no objection. However, if she's there, watch her narrowly, Charles. Lady Freelove is as mischievous as a monkey, and as cunning too. Have a care of her, I say, have a care of her.

CHARLES. If she's there, I'll have her out of the house within this half-hour or set fire to it.

MAJOR O. Nay, now you are too violent—stay a moment, and we'll consider what's best to be done.

Enter OAKLY, *hastily*, R. U. E.

OAKLY. Come, is the coach ready? Let us be gone. Does Charles go with us?

CHARLES. I go with you!—What can I do! I am so vexed and distracted, and so many thoughts crowd in upon me, I don't know which way to turn myself.

MRS. O. (*within*) The coach!—dines out! Where is your master?

OAKLY. Zounds, brother! here she is!

Enter MRS. OAKLY, R. U. E.

MRS. O. (R.) Pray, Mr. Oakly, what is the matter you cannot dine at home to-day?

OAKLY. (R. C.) Don't be uneasy, my dear! I have a little business to settle with my brother; so I am only just going to dinner with him and Charles, to the tavern.

MRS. O. Why cannot you settle your business here, as well as at a tavern? But it is some of your ladies' business, I suppose, and so you must get rid of my company. This chiefly your fault, Major Oakly! (*crosses to him*, R. C.)

MAJOR O. (L. C.) Lord, sister, what signifies it, whether a man dines at home or abroad? (*coolly*)

MRS. O. (R. C.) It signifies a great deal, sir! and I don't choose——

MAJOR O. Phoo! let him go, my dear sister, let him go! he will be ten times better company when he comes back. I tell you what, sister—you sit at home till you are quite tired of one another, and then you grow cross, and fall out. If you would but part a little now and then, you might meet again in humour.

MRS. O. I beg, Major Oakly, that you would trouble yourself about your own affairs; and let me tell you, sir, that I——

OAKLY. Nay, do not put yourself into a passion with the major, my dear!—It is not his fault; and I shall come back to thee very soon.

MRS. O. Come back!—why need you go out? I know well enough when you mean to deceive me; for then there is always a pretence of dining with Sir John, or my lord, or somebody; but when you tell me that you are going to a tavern, it's such a bare-faced affront—— (*crosses to* R.)

OAKLY. (R. C.) This is so strange now! Why, my dear I shall only just——

MRS. O. (R.) Only just go after the lady in the letter, I suppose.

OAKLY. Well, well, I won't go, then. Will that convince you? I'll stay with you, my dear. Will that satisfy you?

MAJOR O. (L. C.) For shame! hold out, if you are a man. (*apart*)

OAKLY. She has been so much vexed this morning already, I must humour her a little now. (*apart*)

MAJOR O. Fie, fie! go out, or you are undone. (*apart*)

OAKLY. You see it's impossible. I'll dine at home with thee, my love. (*apart to* MRS. OAKLY)

MRS. O. Ay, ay, pray do, sir. Dine at a tavern, indeed! (*going*)

OAKLY. (*returning*) You may depend on me another time, major.

MAJOR O. Steel and adamant!—Ah!

MRS. O. (*returning*) Mr. Oakly!

OAKLY. Oh, my dear!

He runs across and goes off with MRS. OAKLY, R. U. E.

MAJOR O. (R.) Ha, ha, ha! there's a picture of resolution! there goes a philosopher for you! ha, Charles!

CHARLES. (L.) O, uncle! I have no spirits to laugh now.

MAJOR O. So! I have a fine time on't between you and my brother. Will you meet me to dinner at the St. Alban's, by four? We'll drink her health, and think of this affair.

CHARLES. Don't depend on me. I shall be running all over the town in pursuit of my Harriet; at all events, I'll go directly to Lady Freelove's. If I find her not there, which way I shall direct myself, heaven knows.

MAJOR O. Harkye, Charles! if you meet with her, you may be at a loss; bring her to my house, and we'll settle the whole affair for you. You shall clap her into a postchaise, take the chaplain of our regiment along with you, wheel her down to Scotland, and when you come back, send to settle her fortune with her father; that's the modern art of making love, Charles! *Exeunt,* L. U. E.

END OF ACT I.

ACT II.

SCENE I.—*Oakly's House. (same scene as Act I.)*

Mrs. OAKLY *discovered seated,* L. C.

MRS. O. After all that letter was certainly intended for my husband. I see plain enough they are all in a plot against me. My husband intriguing, the major working him up to affront me, Charles owning his letters, and so playing into each other's hands. They think me a fool, I find—but I'll be too much for them yet. I have desired to speak with Mr. Oakly, and expect him here immediately. His temper is naturally open ; and if he thinks my anger abated and my suspicions laid asleep, he will certainly betray himself by his behaviour. I'll pretend to believe the fine story they have trumped up, throw him off his guard, and so draw the secret out of him. Here he comes. How hard it is to dissemble one's anger ! Oh, I could rate him soundly ?—but I'll keep down my indignation at present, though it chokes me.

Enter OAKLY, R. U. E.

O, my dear ! I am very glad to see you. Pray sit down ; I longed to see you. It seemed an age till I had an opportunity of talking over the silly affair that happened this morning. (*mildly*)

OAKLY. Why really, my dear——

MRS. O. Nay, don't look so grave now. Come—it's all over. Charles and you have cleared up matters; I am satisfied.

OAKLY. Indeed! You make me happy beyond my expectation. This disposition will ensure our felicity. Do but lay aside your cruel unjust suspicion, and we should never have the least difference. (*they sit,* OAKLY, C., MRS. O., L. C.)

MRS. O. Indeed I begin to think so. I'll endeavour to get the better of it. And really, sometimes it is very ridiculous. My uneasiness this morning, for instance— ha, ha, ha ! To be so much alarmed about the idle letter,

which turned out quite another thing at last. Was not I
very angry with you? Ha, ha, ha! (*affecting a laugh*)

OAKLY. (c.) Don't mention it: let us both forget it.
Your present cheerfulness makes amends for everything.

MRS. O. (L. C.) I am apt to be too violent: I love you too
well to be quite easy about you. (*fondly*) Well, no matter—
what is become of Charles?

OAKLY. Poor fellow! he is on the wing, rambling all
over the town in pursuit of this young lady.

MRS. O. Where is he gone, pray?

OAKLY. First of all, I believe to some of her relations.

MRS. O. Relations! Who are they? where do they live?

OAKLY. There is an aunt of her's lives just in the
neighbourhood—Lady Freelove.

MRS. O. Lady Freelove! Oho! gone to Lady Freelove's, is he? And do you think he will hear anything of
her?

OAKLY. I don't know; but I hope so, with all my soul.

MRS. O. Hope! with all your soul? Do you hope so?
(*alarmed*)

OAKLY. Hope so? Ye—yes;—why, don't you hope
so? (*surprised*)

MRS. O. Why, yes—(*recovering*) Oh, ay, to be sure—
I hope it of all things. You know, my dear, it must give
me great satisfaction, as well as yourself, to see Charles
well settled.

OAKLY. I should think so; and really I don't know
where he can be settled so well. She is a most deserving
young woman, I assure you.

MRS. O. You are well acquainted with her then?

OAKLY. To be sure, my dear, after seeing her so often
last summer, at the major's house in the country, and at
her father's.

MRS. O. So often!

OAKLY. Ay, very often—Charles took care of that—
almost every day.

MRS. O. Indeed! But pray—a—a—I say—a—a——
(*confused*)

OAKLY. What do you say, my dear?

MRS. O. I say—a—a—(*stammering*) Is she handsome?

OAKLY. Prodigiously handsome, indeed.

Mrs. O. Prodigiously handsome! And is she reckoned a sensible girl?

Oakly. A very sensible, modest, agreeable young lady as ever I knew. You would be extremely fond of her, I am sure. You can't imagine how happy I was in her company. Poor Charles! she soon made a conquest of him, and no wonder; she has so many elegant accomplishments; such an infinite fund of cheerfulness and good humour. Why, she's the darling of the whole country.

Mrs. O. You seem quite in raptures about her.

Oakly. Raptures! Not at all. I was only telling you the young lady's character. I thought you would be glad to find that Charles had made so sensible a choice, and was so likely to be happy.

Mrs. O. Oh, Charles? True, as you say, Charles will be mighty happy.

Oakly. Don't you think so?

Mrs. O. I am convinced of it. Poor Charles! I am much concerned for him. He must be very uneasy about her. I was thinking whether we could be of any service to him in this affair.

Oakly. Was you, my love? That is very good of you. Why, to be sure, we must endeavour to assist him. Let me see—how can we manage it? 'Gad! I have hit it. The luckiest thought! and it will be of great service to Charles.

Mrs. O. Well, what is it?—(eagerly)—You know I would do anything to serve Charles, and oblige you. (mildly)

Oakly. That is so kind!—my dear, if you would but always consider things in this proper light, and continue this amiable temper, we should be the happiest people——

Mrs. O. I believe so: but what's your proposal?

Oakly. Charles, you know, may perhaps be so lucky as to meet with this lady——

Mrs. O. True.

Oakly. Now I was thinking, that he might, with your leave, my dear——

Mrs. O. Well!

Oakly. Bring her home here——

Mrs. O. How!

OAKLY. Yes, bring her home, here, my dear;—it will make poor Charles's mind quite easy : and you may take her under your protection till her father comes to town.

MRS. O. Amazing! this is even beyond my expectation.

OAKLY. Why!—what!——

MRS. O. Was there ever such assurance!—(*rises*) Take her under my protection! What! would you keep her under my nose? (*crosses to* R.)

OAKLY. (L.) Nay, I never conceived—I thought you would have approved——

MRS. O. (R.) What!—No place but my own house to serve your purposes!

OAKLY. Lord, this is the strangest misapprehension! I am quite astonished.

MRS. O. Astonished! yes—confused, detected, betrayed, by your vain confidence of imposing on me. Charles, indeed! yes, Charles is a fine excuse for you. The letter this morning, the letter, Mr. Oakly!

OAKLY. The letter! why sure that——

MRS. O. Is sufficiently explained. You have made it very clear to me. Now I am convinced. I have no doubt of your perfidy. But I thank you for some hints you have given me, and you may be sure I shall make use of them ; nor will I rest till I have full conviction, and overwhelm you with the strongest proof of your baseness towards me.

OAKLY. Nay, but—

MRS. O. Go, go! I have no doubt of your falsehood; away !   *Exit,* R. U. E.

OAKLY. Was there ever anything like this? Such unaccountable behaviour! angry I don't know why! jealous of I know not what!—Hints!—hints I have given her!—What can she mean?

Enter TOILET, *crosses the stage, from* R. *to* L.

Toilet! where are you going?

TOILET. To order the porter to let in no company to my lady to-day. She won't see a single soul, sir.

Exit, L.

OAKLY. What an unhappy woman! Now will she sit all day feeding on her suspicions, till she has convinced herself of the truth of them.

Enter JOHN, *crossing the stage from* R. *to* L.

Well, sir, what's your business?

JOHN. Going to order the chariot, sir!—my lady's going out immediately.   *Exit,* L.

OAKLY. Going out! what is all this? But every way she makes me miserable. Wild and ungovernable as the sea or the wind! made up of storms and tempests! I can't bear it; and one way or other I will put an end to it.

                                  Exit, R.

SCENE II.—*Lady Freelove's House.*

Enter LADY FREELOVE, R. *with a card;—a* SERVANT *following.*

LADY F. (*reading as she enters*) "And will take the liberty of waiting on her ladyship *en cavalier.*" Does any body wait that brought this card?

SERVANT. Lord Trinket's servant is in the hall, madam.

LADY F. My compliments, and I shall be glad to see his lordship. Where is Miss Russet?

SERVANT. In her own chamber, madam.

LADY F. What is she doing?

SERVANT. Writing, I believe, madam.

LADY F. Oh, ridiculous!—scribbling to that Oakly, I suppose. (*apart*) Let her know I should be glad of her company here.   *Exit* SERVANT, R.

Oakly must not have her, positively. A match with Lord Trinket will add to the dignity of the family. I must bring her into it. But here she comes.

Enter HARRIET, R. E.

Well, Harriet, still in the pouts! nay, pr'ythee, my dear little runaway girl, be more cheerful!—your everlasting melancholy puts me into the vapours.

HAR. Dear madam, excuse me. How can I be cheerful

in my present situation? I know my father's temper so
well, that I'm sure this step of mine must almost distract
him. I sometimes wish that I had remained in the
country, let what might have been the consequence.

Lady F. Why, it is a naughty child, that's certain;
but it need not be so uneasy about papa, as you know that
I wrote by last night's post, to acquaint him that his little
lost sheep was safe, and that you were ready to obey his
commands in every particular, except marrying that oaf,
Sir Harry Beagle. Well, I don't wonder at your taste;
for to my knowledge you might have a man of quality to-
morrow. Indeed, you have fine eyes, child, and they have
made fine work with Lord Trinket!

Har. Lord Trinket! (*contemptuously*)

Lady F. Yes, Lord Trinket—you know it as well as I
do; and yet, you ill-natured thing, you will not vouchsafe
him a single smile. But you must give the poor soul
a little encouragement, pr'ythee do.

Har. Indeed, I can't, madam, for of all mankind, Lord
Trinket is my aversion.

Lady F. Indeed, my dear, this affectation sits very
awkwardly upon you. There will be a superiority in the
behaviour of persons of fashion.

Har. A superiority, indeed! for his lordship always
behaves with the most insolent familiarity.

Lady F. Innocent freedoms, child, which every fine
woman expects to be taken with her, as an acknowledg-
ment of her beauty.

Har. They are freedoms which I think no innocent
woman can allow.

Lady F. Romantic to the last degree!—Why, you are
in the country still, Harriet!

Enter a Servant, l.

Serv. My lord Trinket, madam.   *Exit*, l.

Lady F. I swear now, I have a good mind to tell him
all that you have said.

Enter Lord Trinket, l.

Your lordship's most obedient, humble servant.

LORD T. Your ladyship does me too much honor. Miss Russet, I am your slave. I declare it makes me quite happy to find you together. 'Pon honor, ma'am, —(*to* HARRIET) I begin to conceive great hopes of you; and as for you, Lady Freelove, I cannot sufficiently commend your assiduity with your fair pupil. By-the-bye, I met a monster at the riding-house this morning, who gave me some intelligence that will surprise you, concerning your family.

HAR. What intelligence?

LADY F. Who was this monster, as your lordship calls him? A curiosity, I dare say!

LORD T. This monster, madam, was formerly my head groom, and had the care of all my running horses.

HAR. Dear, my lord, don't talk of your groom, but tell me the news. Do you know anything of my father?

LORD T. Your father, madam, is now in town. This fellow, you must know, is now groom to Sir Harry Beagle, your sweet rural swain, and informed me that his master and your father were running all over the town in quest of you; and that he himself had orders to enquire after you; for which reason, I suppose he came to the riding-house stable to look after a horse, thinking it, to be sure, a very likely place to meet you. Your father, perhaps, is gone to seek you at the Tower, or Westminster Abbey, which is all the idea he has of London; and your faithful lover is probably cheapening a hunter, and drinking strong beer at the Horse and Jockey, in Smithfield.

LADY F. The whole set admirably disposed of!

HAR. Did not your lordship inform him where I was?

LORD T. Not I, 'pon honor, madam; that I left to their own ingenuity to discover.

LADY F. And pray, my lord, where in this town, have this polite company bestowed themselves?

LORD T. They lodge, madam, of all places in the world, at the Bull and Gate Inn, in Holborn.

LADY F. Ha, ha, ha! The Bull and Gate!—incomparable! What have they brought any hay or cattle to town?

LORD T. Very well, Lady Freelove, very well, indeed.

There they are, like so many graziers; and there it seems they have learned that this lady is certainly in London.

HAR. Do, dear madam, send a card directly to my father, informing him where I am, and that your ladyship would be glad to see him here. For my part, I dare not venture into his presence, till you have in some measure pacified him; but for heaven's sake, desire him not to bring that wretched fellow along with him.

LORD T. Wretched fellow! Oho! Courage, Milor Trinket! (*aside*)

LADY F. I'll send immediately. Who's there?

Re-enter SERVANT, L.

SERVANT. (*apart to* LADY F.) Sir Harry Beagle is below, madam.

LADY F. (*apart to* SERVANT) I am not at home. Have they let him in?

SERVANT. Yes, madam.

LADY F. How abominably unlucky this is! Well, then show him into my dressing room, I will come to him there.   *Exit* SERVANT, L.

LORD T. Lady Freelove! no engagement, I hope? We won't part with you, 'pon honor.

LADY F. The worst engagement in the world. A pair of musty old prudes! Lady Formal and Miss Prate.

LORD T. O, the beldames! As nauseous as ipecacuanha, 'pon honor.

LADY F. Lud, lud! what shall I do with them? Why do these foolish women come troubling me now? I must wait on them in the dressing room. Harriet, you'll entertain his lordship till I return.

Exit, L.

LORD T. Gone! 'Pon honor, I am not sorry for the coming in of these old tabbies, and am much obliged to her ladyship for leaving us to such an agreeable tête-a-tête.

HAR. Your lordship will find me extremely bad company.

LORD T. Not in the least, my dear. We'll entertain ourselves one way or other, I'll warrant you. 'Egad, I think it a mighty good opportunity to establish a better acquaintance with you.

HAR. I don't understand you.

LORD T. No? Why, then I'll speak plainer. (*pausing, and looking her full in the face*) You are an amazing fine creature, 'pon honor.

HAR. If this be your lordship's polite conversation, I shall leave you to amuse yourself in soliloquy. (*going*)

LORD T. No, no, no, madam, that must not be. (*stopping her*) This place, my passion, the opportunity, all conspire—

HAR. How, sir! you don't intend to do me any violence?

LORD T. 'Pon honor, ma'am, it will be doing great violence to myself, if I do not. You must excuse me. (*struggling with her*)

HAR. Help, help! Murder! Help!

LORD T. Your yelping will signify nothing—nobody will come. (*struggling*)

HAR. For heaven's sake!—Sir! My lord! (*noise within*)

LORD T. Plague on't, what a noise! Then I must be quick. (*still struggling*)

HAR. Help! Murder! Help, help!

Enter CHARLES, *hastily,* L.

CHARLES. (*seeing them*) Is it possible? Turn, ruffian! I'll find you employment. (*drawing*)

LORD T. You are a most impertinent scoundrel! and I'll whip you through the lungs, 'pon honor. (*they fight*)

HARRIET *runs out, screaming* "Help!" *&c.,* R.

Re-enter LADY FREELOVE, *with* SIR HARRY BEAGLE, L.

LADY F. How's this? Swords drawn in my house! Part them. (*they are parted*) This is the most impudent thing——

LORD T. Well, rascal, I shall find a time. I know you, sir.

CHARLES. The sooner the better. I know your lordship too.

SIR H. I'faith, madam, (*to* LADY FREELOVE) we had like to have been in at the death.

LADY F. What is all this? Pray, sir, what is the meaning of your coming hither to raise this disturbance? Who are you? What brought you here?

CHARLES. I am one, madam, always ready to draw my sword in defence of innocence in distress, and more especially in the cause of that lady I delivered from his lordship's fury, in search of whom I troubled your ladyship's house.

LADY F. Her lover, I suppose; or what?

CHARLES. At your ladyship's service; though not quite so violent in my passion as his lordship there.

LORD T. Impertinent rascal!

LADY F. You shall be made to repent of this insolence.

LORD T. Your ladyship may leave that to me.

CHARLES. Ha, ha!

SIR H. But pray what is become of the lady all this while? Why, Lady Freelove, you told me she was not here; and i'faith, I was just drawing off another way, it I had not heard the view-halloo.

LADY F. You shall see her immediately, sir. Who's there?

(SIR HARRY *crosses behind to* R.)

Enter SERVANT, L.

Where is Miss Russet?

SERVANT. Gone out, Madam.

LADY F. Gone out? Where?

SERVANT. I don't know, Madam; but she ran down the back stairs, crying for help, crossed the servants' hall in tears, and took a chair at the door.

LADY F. Blockheads! to let her go out in a chair alone! Go and enquire after her immediately. *Exit* SERVANT, L.

SIR H. Gone!—When I had just run her down! and is the little puss stole away at last?

LADY F. Sir, if you will walk in (*to* SIR H.) with his lordship and me, perhaps you may hear some tidings of her; though it is most probable she may be gone to her father. I don't know any other friend she has in town.

CHARLES. I am heartily glad she is gone. She is safer anywhere than in this house. (L. *corner*)

LADY F. (L. C.) Mighty well, sir! Sir Harry, I attend you.

LORD T. (R. C.) You shall hear from me, sir! (*to* CHARLES)

CHARLES. (L.) Very well, my lord.

SIR H. Stole away!—plague on't—stole away!

Exit SIR HARRY, R. 1 E.

LADY F. Before you go, give me leave to tell you, sir, that your behaviour here has been so extraordinary——

CHARLES. My treatment here, madam, has indeed been very extraordinary.

LADY F. Indeed! Well, no matter—permit me to acquaint you, sir, that there lies your way out, and that the greatest favor you can do me, is to leave the house immediately.

CHARLES. That your ladyship may depend on.   Since you have put Miss Russet to flight, you may be sure of not being troubled with my company. I'll after her immediately.

LADY F. If she has any regard for her reputation, she'll never put herself into such hands as yours.

CHARLES. O, madam, there can be no doubt of her regard for that, by her leaving your ladyship.

LADY F. Leave my house.

CHARLES. Directly—a charming house ; and a charming lady of the house too!—Ha, ha, ha!

LADY F. Vulgar fellow !

CHARLES. Fine lady !   *Exit* CHARLES, L.

LADY F. (L.) Indeed, indeed, my Lord Trinket, this is absolutely intolerable !   What, to offer rudeness to a young lady in my house !   What will the world say of it?

LORD T. (R.) Just what the world pleases : it does not signify a doit what they say.   However, I ask pardon ; but, 'egad, I thought it was the best way.

LADY F. As this is rather an ugly affair, and may make some noise, I think it absolutely necessary, merely to save appearances, that you should wait on her father, palliate matters as well as you can, and make a formal repetition of your proposal of marriage.

LORD T. Your ladyship is perfectly in the right.   You are quite *au fait* of the affair.   It shall be done immediately, and then your reputation will be safe, and my conduct justified to all the world.   But should the old rustic continue as stubborn as his daughter, your ladyship, I hope, has no objection to my being a little *rusée*, for I must have her, 'pon honor.

Enter SERVANT, L.

SERVANT. (L.) Mrs. Oakly, madam, is at the door, in her chariot, and desires to have the honor of speaking to your ladyship on particular business.

Lord T. (r.) Mrs. Oakly! What can that jealous-pated woman want with you?

Lady F. (c.) No matter what. I hate her mortally. Let her in. *Exit* Servant, L.

Lord T. What wind blows her hither?

Lady F. A wind that must blow us some good.

Lord T. How? I was amazed you chose to see her.

Lady F. How can you be so slow of apprehension? She comes, you may be sure, on some occasion relating to this girl, in order to assist young Oakly; perhaps, to soothe me, and gain intelligence, and so forward the match; but I'll forbid the banns, I warrant you. Whatever she wants, I'll draw some sweet mischief out of it. But away, away! I think I hear her. Slip down the back stairs—or stay— now I think on't, go out this way—meet her—and be sure to make her a very respectful bow as you go out.

Lord T. Hush! here she is. (*crosses to* L.)

Enter Mrs. Oakly, L. Lord Trinket *bows and exit*, L. Servant *re-enters, places chairs, and exit*, L.

Mrs. O. (L.) I beg pardon, for **giving your** ladyship this trouble.

Lady F. (r.) I am always glad of the honor of seeing Mrs. Oakly.

Mrs. O. There is a letter, madam, just come from the country, which has occasioned some alarm in our family. It comes from Mr. Russet——

Lady F. Mr. Russet! (*they sit*)

Mrs. O. Yes, from Mr. Russet, madam; and is chiefly concerning his daughter. As she has the honour of being related to your ladyship, I took the liberty of waiting on you.

Lady F. She is indeed, as you say, madam, a relation of mine; but after what has happened, I scarce know how to acknowledge her.

Mrs. O. Has she been so much to blame, then?

Lady F. So much, madam! Only judge for yourself. Though she had been so indiscreet, not to say indecent in her conduct, as to elope from her father, I was in hopes to have hushed up that matter, for the honor of our family; but she has run away from me too, madam—went off in the most abrupt manner, not an hour ago.

Mrs. O. You surprise me. Indeed, her father, by his
letter, seems apprehensive of the worst consequences.
But does your ladyship imagine any harm has happened?

Lady F. I can't tell—I hope not; but indeed she's a
strange girl. You know, madam, young women can't be
too cautious in their conduct. She is—I am sorry to
declare it—a very dangerous person to take into a family.

Mrs. O. Indeed! (*alarmed*)

Lady F. If I was to say all I know——

Mrs. O. Why sure your ladyship knows of nothing
that has been carried on clandestinely between her and
Mr. Oakly? (*in disorder*)

Lady F. Mr: Oakly?

Mrs. O. Mr. Oakly? No, not Mr. Oakly—that is, not
my husband—I don't mean him—not him, but his nephew
—young Mr. Oakly.

Lady F. Jealous of her husband. So, so—now I know
my game. (*aside*)

Mrs. O. But pray, madam, give me leave to ask, was
there anything very particular in her conduct while she
was in your ladyship's house?

Lady F. Why, really, considering she was here scarce
a week, her behaviour was rather mysterious;—letters and
messages, to and fro, between her and I don't know who.
I suppose you know that Mr. Oakly's nephew has been
here, madam?

Mrs. O. I was not sure of it. Has he been to wait on
your ladyship on this occasion?

Lady F. To wait on me! The expression is much too
polite for the nature of the visit. My Lord Trinket, the
nobleman whom you met as you came in, had, you must
know, madam, some thoughts of my niece, and, as it would
have been an advantageous match, I was glad of it; but
I believe, after what he has been witness to this morning,
he will drop all thoughts of it.

Mrs. O. I am sorry that any relation of mine should so
far forget himself——

Lady F. It's no matter. His behaviour, indeed, as well
as the young lady's, was pretty extraordinary; and yet,
after all, I don't believe he is the object of her affections.

Mrs. O. Ha! (*much alarmed*)

LADY F. She has certainly an attachment somewhere, a strong one; but his lordship, who was present all the time, was convinced, as well as myself, that Mr. Oakly's nephew was rather a convenient friend, a kind of go-between, than the lover. Bless me, madam, you change colour!—you seem uneasy! What's the matter?

MRS. O. Nothing, madam—nothing—a little shocked that my husband should behave so.

LADY F. Your husband, madam!

MRS. O. His nephew, I mean. His unpardonable rudeness—but I am not well. I am sorry to have given your ladyship so much trouble. (*rises*) I'll take my leave.

LADY F. I declare, madam, you frighten me. Your being so visibly affected makes me quite uneasy. I hope I have not said any thing—I really don't believe your husband is in fault. Men, to be sure, allow themselves strange liberties—but I think, nay, I am sure, it cannot be so, it is impossible! Don't let what I have said have any effect on you.

MRS. O. No, it has not—I have no idea of such a thing. Your ladyship's most obedient. (*going—returns*) But, sure, madam, you have not heard—or don't know any thing?

LADY F. Come, come, Mrs. Oakly, I see how it is, and it would not be kind to say all I know. I dare not tell you what I have heard. Only be on your guard—there can be no harm in that. Do you be against giving the girl any countenance, and see what effect it has.

MRS. O. I will—I am much obliged. (*going—returns*) But does it appear to your ladyship, then, that Mr. Oakly—

LADY F. No, not at all—nothing in't, I dare say—I would not create uneasiness in a family—but I am a woman myself, have been married, and can't help feeling for you. But don't be uneasy; there's nothing in't I dare say.

MRS. O. I think so. Your ladyship's humble servant. (*curtseying*)

LADY F. Your servant, madam. Pray don't be alarmed: I must insist on your not making yourself uneasy.

MRS. O. Not at all alarmed—not in the least uneasy— your most obedient servant. Oh, Mr. Oakley!

Exit, L.

LADY F. Ha, ha, ha! There she goes brimfull of anger

and jealousy, to vent it all on her husband.   Mercy on the
poor man !   *Exit* LADY FREELOVE, R. 1 E.

SCENE III.—*Mr. Oakly's House.*

Enter HARRIET, L. U. E., *following* JOHN.

HAR. (L.) Not at home!   Are you sure that Mrs. Oakly
is not at home ?

JOHN. (R.) She is just gone out, madam.

HAR. I have something of consequence.   If you will
give me leave, I will wait till she returns.

JOHN. You would not see her, if you did, madam.   She
has given positive orders not to be interrupted with any
company to-day.

HAR. Sure, if you was to let her know that I had particular business——

JOHN. I should not dare to trouble her indeed, madam.

HAR. How unfortunate this is!—what can I do?   Pray,
can I see Mr. Oakly then ?

JOHN. Yes, madam : I'll acquaint my master, if you
please.

HAR. Pray do.

JOHN. Will you favor me with your name, madam ?

HAR. Be pleased to let him know that a lady desires
to speak with him.

JOHN. I shall, madam.   *Exit*, R. U. E.

HAR. I wish I could have seen Mrs. Oakly.   What an
unhappy situation I am reduced to by my father's obstinate
perseverance to force me into a marriage which my soul
abhors.

Enter OAKLY, R. U. E.

OAKLY. (R., *at entering*) Where is this lady? (*seeing her*
—*places chair for her,* C.) Bless me, Miss Russet, is it
you?   Was ever anything so unlucky. (*aside*)   Is it
possible, madam, that I see you here ?

HAR. (L.) It is too true, sir; and the occasion on which
I am now to trouble you, is so much in need of an apology,
that——(*sits,* L. C.)

OAKLY. Pray make none, madam.   If my wife should
return before I get her out of the house again ! (*aside*)

D

HAR. I dare say, sir, you are not quite a stranger to the attachment your nephew has professed to me.

OAKLY. I am not, madam: I hope Charles has not been guilty of any baseness towards you. If he has, I'll never see his face again.

HAR. I have no cause to accuse him—but——

OAKLY. But what, madam?—pray be quick! The very person in the world I would not have seen! (*aside*)

HAR. You seem uneasy, sir.

OAKLY. No—nothing at all. (*sits*, R. C.) Pray go on, madam.

HAR. I am at present, sir, through a concurrence of strange accidents, in a very unfortunate situation, and do not know what will become of me without your assistance.

OAKLY. I'll do everything in my power to serve you: I know of your leaving your father, by a letter we have had from him. Pray let me know the rest of your story.

HAR. My story, sir, is very short.

OAKLY. (*aside*) Thank heaven!

HAR. When I left my father's, I came immediately to London, and took refuge with a relation; where, instead of meeting with the protection I expected, I was alarmed with the most infamous designs. It is not an hour ago since your nephew rescued me from a villain. I tremble to think that I left him actually engaged in a duel.

OAKLY. He is very safe. He has just sent home the chariot, from the St. Alban's tavern, where he dines to-day.—But what are your commands for me, madam?

HAR. The favour, sir, I would now request of you is, that you would suffer me to remain, for a days, in your house.

OAKLY. Madam!

HAR. And that, in the mean time, you will use your utmost endeavours to reconcile me to my father.

OAKLY. This is the most perplexing situation! Why did not Charles take care to bestow you properly?

HAR. It is most probable, sir, that I should not have consented to such measure myself. The world is but too apt to censure, even without a cause: and if you are so kind as to admit me into your house. I must desire not to consider Mr. Oakly in any other light than as your nephew.

OAKLY. What an unlucky circumstance!—(*aside*) Upon my soul, madam, I would do anything to serve you—but being in my house creates a difficulty, that——

HAR. I hope, sir, you do not doubt the truth of what I have told you?

OAKLY. I religiously believe every tittle of it, madam; but I have particular family considerations, that——

HAR. Sure, sir, you cannot suspect me to be base enough to form any connexions in your family contrary to your inclinations, while I am living in your house!

OAKLY. Such connexions, madam, would do me and all my family great honour. I never dreamt of any scruples on that account.—What can I do?—Let me see—let me see—suppose. (*pausing*)

Enter MRS. OAKLY *through* C. D. *in a carriage dress.*

MRS. O. I am sure I heard the voice of a woman, conversing with my husband—Ha! (*seeing* HARRIET) It is so indeed! Let me contain myself—I'll listen. (*aside*)

HAR. I see, sir, you are not inclined to serve me—good heaven! what am I reserved to?—Why, why did I leave my father's house, to expose myself to greater distresses?
(*ready to weep*)

OAKLY. I would do anything for your sake, indeed I would. So pray be comforted, and I'll think of some proper place to bestow you in.

MRS. O. So! so!

HAR. What place can be so proper as your own house?

OAKLY. My dear madam, I—I——

MRS. O. My dear madam!—Mighty well!— (*aside—closes door*)

OAKLY. Hush!—hark—what noise?

HAR. I heard no noise.

OAKLY. I did though. (OAKLY *rises, goes to each door, listens and returns to his seat*) No, nothing. But I'll be plain with you, madam; we may be interrupted.—The family consideration I hinted at is nothing else than my wife. She is a little unhappy in her temper, madam;—

and if you were to be admitted into the house, I don't know what would be the consequence.

MRS. O. Very fine! (*aside*)

HAR. My behaviour, sir!——

OAKLY. My dear life, it would be impossible for you to behave in such a manner as not to give her suspicion.

HAR. But if your nephew, sir, took everything upon himself——

OAKLY. Still that would not do, madam. Why, this very morning, when the letter came from your father, though I positively denied any knowledge of it, and Charles owned it, yet it was almost impossible to pacify her.

HAR. What shall I do?—What will become of me?

OAKLY. Why, look ye, my dear madam, since my wife is so strong an objection, it is absolutely impossible for me to take you into the house. Nay, if I had not known she was gone out, just before you came, I should be uneasy at your being here, even now. So we must manage as well as we can. I'll take a private lodging for you, a little way off, unknown to Charles, or my wife, or anybody; and if Mrs. Oakly should discover it at last, why the whole matter will light upon Charles, you know.

MRS. O. (*aside*) Upon Charles!

HAR. How unhappy is my situation!—(*weeping*)—I am ruined for ever.

OAKLY. Ruined! Not at all. Such a thing as this has happened to many a young lady before you, and all has been well again. Keep up your spirits! I'll contrive, if I possibly can, to visit you every day.

MRS. O. (C. *advances*) Will you so? O, Mr. Oakly! have I discovered you at last? I'll visit you, indeed! And you, my dear madam, I'll——

HAR. (L.) Madam, I don't understand——

MRS. O. I understand the whole affair, and have understood it for some time past. You shall have a private lodging, miss! It is the fittest place for you, I believe. How dare you look me in the face?

OAKLY. (R.) For heaven's sake, my love, don't be so violent. You are quite wrong in this affair—you don't know who you are talking to. This lady is a person of **fashion.**

Mrs. O. Fine fashion, indeed! to seduce other women's husbands!

Har. Dear madam, how can you imagine——

Oakly. I tell you, my dear, this is the young lady that
Charles——

Mrs. O. Mighty well! but that won't do, sir!—Did not
I hear you lay the whole intrigue together? Did not I hear
your fine plot of throwing all the blame upon Charles?——

Oakly. Nay, be cool a moment. You must know, my
dear, that the letter which came this morning related to
this lady——

Mrs. O. I know it.

Oakly. And since that, it seems, Charles has been so
fortunate as to——

Mrs. O. O, you deceitful man!—That trick is too stale
to pass again with me. It is plain now what you meant
by your proposing to take her into the house this morning.
But the gentlewoman could introduce herself, I see.

Oakly. Fie! fie! my dear, she came on purpose to in-
quire for you.

Mrs. O. For me!—better and better!—Did not she
watch her opportunity, and come to you just as I went
out? But I am obliged to you for your visit, madam.
It is sufficiently paid. Pray don't let me detain you.

Oakly. For shame, for shame, Mrs. Oakly! How can
you be so absurd? Is this proper behaviour to a lady of
her character?

Mrs. O. I have heard her character. Go, my fine, runaway madam! Now you have eloped from your family,
and run away from your aunt!—Go!—You shan't stay
here, I promise you. (crosses to R.)

Oakly. (c.) Pr'ythee be quiet. You don't know what
you are doing. She shall stay.

Mrs. O. She shan't stay a minute.

Oakly. She shall stay a minute, an hour, a day, a week,
a month, a year!—'Sdeath, madam, she shall stay for ever
if I choose it.

Mrs. O. How!

Har. For heaven's sake, sir, let me go. I am frightened
to death.

Oakly. Don't be afraid, madam. She shall stay, I insist
upon it.

RUSSET. (*within*) I tell you, sir, I will go up. I am sure the lady is here, and nothing shall hinder me.

HAR. O, my father! my father! (*faints*)

OAKLY. See, she faints!—(*catches her*)—Ring the bell! Who's there?

MRS. O. What!—take her into your arms, too!—I have no patience.

Enter RUSSET, L.

RUSSET. (L.) Where is this—ha, fainting!—(*runs to her*) O, my dear Harriet! my child, my child!

OAKLY. (C.) Your coming so abruptly shocked her spirits. But she revives. How do you do, madam?

HAR. (*to* RUSSET) O, sir!

RUSSET. O, my dear girl, how could you run away from your father, that loves you with such fondness? But I was sure I should find you here——

MRS. O. (R.) There, there!—sure he should find her here! Did I not tell you so?—Are not you a wicked man, to carry on such base underhand doings with a gentleman's daughter?

RUSSET. (*crosses to* L. C.) Look you, Mr. Oakly, I shall expect satisfaction from your family for so gross an affront. How durst you encourage my daughter to an elopement, and receive her in your house? Zounds, sir, I am not to be used ill by any man in England.

OAKLY. (C.) Sir, this is all a mistake.

RUSSET. (L. C.) A mistake! Did not I find her in your house?

OAKLY. Upon my soul she has not been in my house above——

MRS. O. (R. C.) Did not I hear you say you would take her a lodging—a private lodging?

OAKLY. (C.) Yes, but that——

RUSSET. Has not this affair been carried on a long time, in spite of my teeth?

OAKLY. Sir, I never troubled myself——

MRS. O. Never troubled yourself!—Did not you insist on her staying in the house, whether I would or no?

OAKLY. No,

RUSSET. Did not you send to meet her, when she came to town?

OAKLY. No.

MRS. O. Did not you deceive me about the letter this morning?

OAKLY. No—no—no—I tell you, no!

MRS. O. Yes—yes—yes—I tell you, yes!

(they all go up and down the stage)

RUSSET. Shan't I believe my own eyes?

MRS. O. Shan't I believe my own ears?

OAKLY. 'Sdeath, you will not let me speak! and you are both alike, I think: I wish you were married to one another, with all my heart.

MRS. O. Mighty well! mighty well!

RUSSET. I shall soon find a time to talk with you.

OAKLY. Find a time to talk! you have talked enough now for all your lives.

MRS. O. Very fine! Come along, sir; leave that lady with her father. Now she is in the properest hands.

Exit, R. U. E.

OAKLY. I wish I could leave you in his hands. *(going* R. U. E.—*returns)* One word with you, sir. The height of your passion, and Mrs. Oakly's strange misapprehension of this whole affair, makes it impossible to explain matters to you at present. I will do it when you please, and how you please.

RUSSET. Yes, yes! I'll have satisfaction. So, madam, I have found you at last: you have made a fine confusion here.

HAR. My dear sir, you misunderstand the whole affair. I have not been in this house half an hour.

RUSSET. Zounds, girl, don't put me in a passion! You know I love you, but a lie puts me in a passion. But come along—we'll leave this house directly.

Exit RUSSET *and* HARRIET, L. D.

END OF ACT II.

———————————

ACT III.

SCENE I.—*Mrs. Oakly's Dressing Room.*

MRS. OAKLY *discovered seated at table*, R. C.

MRS. O. This is worse and worse! He never held me so much in contempt before—to go out without speaking to me, or taking the least notice. I am obliged to the major for this. How could he take him out! and how could Mr. Oakly go with him!

Enter TOILET, L. U. E.

Well, Toilet?

TOILET. My master is not come back yet, ma'am.

MRS. O. Where is he gone?

TOILET. I don't know, I can assure your ladyship.

MRS. O. Why don't you know?—you know nothing—but I warrant you know well enough if you would tell. You shall never persuade me but you knew of Mr. Oakly's going out to-day.

TOILET. I wish I may die, ma'am, upon my honour, and I protest to your ladyship I know nothing in the world of the matter, no more than the child unborn.

MRS. O. He is certainly gone after this young flirt. His confidence and the major's insolence provoke me beyond expression. Bid John come to me—Toilet!

TOILET. Ma'am.

MRS. O. Where's John? Why don't he come? Why do you stand with your hands before you? Why don't you fetch him?

TOILET. Yes, ma'am, I'll go this minute. O—here, John—my lady wants you. (*goes to door*, L. U. E.)

Enter JOHN, L. U. E.

MRS. O. Where's your master?

JOHN. Gone out, madam.

MRS. O. Why did not you go with him?

JOHN. Because he went out in the major's chariot, madam.

MRS. O. Where did they go to?

JOHN. To the major's, I suppose, madam.

MRS. O. Suppose! Don't you know.

JOHN. I believe so, but I can't tell for certain, indeed, madam.

MRS. O. Believe and suppose—and don't know, and can't tell! You are all fools! Go about your business. (JOHN *going*) Come here! (*returns*) Go to the major's— no—it does not signify—go along! (JOHN *going*) Yes, harkye, (*returns*) go to the major's, and see if your master is there.

JOHN. Give your compliments, madam?

MRS. O. My compliments, blockhead! Get along! (JOHN *going*) Come hither! (*he returns*) Can't you go to the major's, and bring me word if Mr. Oakly is there, without taking any further notice?

JOHN. Yes, ma'am.

MRS. O. Well, why don't you go then? And make haste back—and, d'ye hear, John? (JOHN *going, returns*)

JOHN. Madam!

MRS. O. Nothing at all—go along. (JOHN *goes*) How uneasy Mr. Oakly makes me! Harkye, John! (JOHN *returns*)

JOHN. Madam!

MRS. O. Send the porter here.

JOHN. Yes, madam.   *Exit,* L.

TOILET. So, she's in a rare humour! I shall have a fine time on't. (*aside*) Will your ladyship choose to dress?

MRS. O. Pr'ythee, creature, don't tease me with your fiddle-faddle stuff—I have a thousand things to think of. Where is the porter? why has not that booby sent him? What is the meaning——

Re-enter JOHN, L.

JOHN. Madam, my master has this moment returned, with Major Oakly, and my young master, and the lady that was here yesterday.

MRS. O. Very well.   *Exit* JOHN, L.

Returned—yes, truly, he is returned. This is setting me at open defiance. But I'll go down, and show them I have too much spirit to endure such usage. (*going*) Or, stay— I'll not go amongst his company —I'll go out—Toilet!

TOILET. Ma'am.

MRS. O. Order the coach; I'll go out. (TOILET *going)* Toilet, stay—I'll e'en go down to them. No—Toilet!

TOILET. Ma'am.

MRS. O. Order me a boiled chicken—I'll not go down to dinner; I'll dine in my own room, and sup there. I'll not see his face these three days.   *Exeunt,* R.

SCENE II.—*Room in Oakly's House.*

Enter OAKLY, MAJOR OAKLY, CHARLES, *and* HARRIET, L.

OAKLY. (c.) Be comforted, madam; we shall soon hear of Mr. Russet, and all will be well, I dare say.

Re-enter TOILET, R.

Well, Toilet, what now? (TOILET *whispers him*) Not well? Can't come down to dinner? Wants to see me above? Harkye, brother—what shall I do?

MAJOR O. (L. C.) If you go, you are undone.

HAR. (L.) Go, sir—go to Mrs. Oakly; indeed you had better.

MAJOR O. 'Sdeath, brother! don't budge a foot. This is all fractiousness and ill humour.

OAKLY. No, I'll not go. Tell her I have company, and we shall be glad to see her here.

Exit TOILET, R.

MAJOR O. That's right.

OAKLY. Suppose I go and watch how she proceeds?

MAJOR O. What d'ye mean? You would not go to her? Are you mad?

OAKLY. By no means go to her—I only want to know how she takes it. I'll lie perdue in my study, and observe her motions.

MAJOR O. I don't like this pitiful ambuscade work—this bush fighting. Why can't you stay here? Ay, ay! I know how it will be. She'll come bounce in upon you with a torrent of anger and passion, or, if necessary, a whole flood of tears, and carry all before her at once.

OAKLY. You shall find that you are mistaken, major.

Now I am convinced I'm in the right, I'll support that right with ten times your steadiness.

MAJOR O. You talk this well, brother.

OAKLY. I'll do it well, brother.

MAJOR O. If you don't, you are undone.

OAKLY. Never fear, never fear.   *Exit*, R.

MAJOR O. Well, Charles?

CHARLES. I'll go immediately in quest of Mr. Russet. Perhaps I may learn at the inn where his lordship's ruffians have carried him.

RUSSET. (*without*, L.) Here! Yes, yes, I know she's here, well enough. Come along, Sir Harry—come along.

HAR. He's here—my father! I know his voice. Where is Mr. Oakly? Oh, now, good sir, (*to the* MAJOR) do but pacify him, and you'll be a friend indeed.

Enter RUSSET, LORD TRINKET, *and* SIR HARRY BEAGLE, L.

LORD T. (L.) There, sir—I told you it was so.

RUSSET. (L. C.) Ay, ay, it is too plain. Oh, you provoking slut! Elopement after elopement! and at last to have your father carried off by violence—to endanger my life! Zounds! I am so angry I dare not trust myself within reach of you.

CHARLES. (R. C.) I can assure you, sir, that your daughter is entirely——

RUSSET. You assure me! You are the fellow that has perverted her mind—that has set my own child against me——

CHARLES. If you will but hear me, sir——

RUSSET. I won't hear a word you say. I'll have my daughter—I won't hear a word.

MAJOR O. (R.) Nay, Mr. Russet, hear reason. If you will but have patience——

RUSSET. I'll have no patience, I'll have my daughter, and she shall marry Sir Harry to-night. Take her away, Sir Harry; she shall marry you to-night.

MAJOR O. Only three words, Mr. Russet——

RUSSET. Why don't the booby take her?

SIR H. Hold hard! Hold hard! You are all on a wrong scent. Hold hard! I say, hold hard!—Hark ye, 'Squire Russet,

Russet. Well, what now?

Sir H. It was proposed, you know, to match me with Miss Harriet—but she can't take kindly to me.—When one has made a bad bet, it is best to hedge off, you know—and so I have e'en swapped her with Lord Trinket here, for his brown horse, Nabob.

Russet. Swapped her! Swapped my daughter for a horse! Zounds, sir, what d'ye mean?

Sir H. Mean? Why, I mean to be off, to be sure—it won't do—I tell you it won't do. First of all I knocked up myself and my horses, when they took for London, and now I have been stewed aboard a tender. I have wasted three stone at least. If I could have rid my match it would not have grieved me; and so, as I said before, I have swapped her for Nabob.

Russet. The devil take Nabob, and yourself, and Lord Trinket, and——

Lord T. Pardon! je vous demande pardon, Monsieur Russet, 'pon honour.

Russet. Death and the devil! I shall go distracted! My daughter plotting against me—the——

Major O. (crosses to R. C.) Come, come, Mr. Russet, I am your man, after all. Give me but a moment's hearing, and I'll engage to make peace between you and your daughter, and throw the blame where it ought to fall most deservedly.

Sir H. (L.) Ay, ay, that's right. Put the saddle on the right horse, my buck!

Russet. Well, sir—what d'ye say? Speak—I don't know what to do.

Major O. I'll speak the truth, let who will be offended by it. I have proof presumptive and positive for you, Mr. Russet. From his lordship's behaviour at Lady Freelove's, when my nephew rescued her, we may fairly conclude that he would stick at no measures to carry his point—there's proof presumptive. But, sir, we can give you proof positive too;—proof under his lordship's own hand, that he likewise was the contriver of this last plot to waylay you and Sir Harry Beagle, and induced a pressgang to carry you on board their tender; in short, planned entirely the gross affront that has just been offered you.

RUSSET. Hey! how?

LORD T. Every syllable romance, 'pon honour.

MAJOR O. Gospel, every word on't.

CHARLES. (crosses to L. C.) This letter will convince you, sir. In consequence of what happened at Lady Free-love's, his lordship thought fit to send me a challenge; but the messenger blundered, and gave me this letter instead of it. (giving the letter) I have the case which enclosed it in my pocket. (goes back to R.)

LORD T. Forgery from beginning to end, 'pon honour.

MAJOR O. Truth, upon my honour. But read, read, Mr. Russet, read, and be convinced.

RUSSET. Let me see, let me see. (reads) Um—um—um—um—so, so—um—um—um—damnation! "Wish me success—obedient slave, Trinket." Fire and fury! How dare you do this?

LORD T. When you are cool, Mr. Russet, I will explain this matter to you.

RUSSET. (L. C.) Cool? 'Sdeath and fire—I'll never be cool again!—I'll be revenged! So my Harriet, my dear girl, is innocent at last. Say so, my Harriet; tell me you are innocent. (embraces, &c.)

HAR. (C.) I am indeed, sir, and happy beyond expression at your being convinced of it.

RUSSET. I am glad on't—I am glad on't; I believe you, Harriet: you was always a good girl.

MAJOR O. (R. C.) So she is, an excellent girl; worth a regiment of such lords and baronets. Come, sir, finish everything handsomely at once; come, Charles will have a handsome fortune.

RUSSET. Marry!—she durst not do it!

MAJOR O. Consider, sir, they have long been fond of each other; old acquaintance—faithful lovers—turtles—and may be very happy.

RUSSET. Well, well—since things are so—I love my girl. Harkye, young Oakly, if you don't make a good husband, you'll break my heart, you rogue.

MAJOR O. (R.) I'll cut his throat if he don't.

CHARLES. (R. C.) Do not doubt it, sir; my Harriet has reformed me altogether.

5

RUSSET. Has she? Why, then—there, heaven bless
you both; there—now there's an end on't.

SIR H. (L.) So, my lord, you and I are both distanced—
a hollow thing, demme.

LORD T. (L.) N'importe.

SIR H. Now this stake is drawn, my lord may be for
hedging off, mayhap. Ecod! I'll go to Jack Speeds,
secure Nabob, and be out of town in an hour. (*aside*)

Exit, L.

LORD T. Well, as matters are so settled, why I wish you
joy, that's all. If Mademoiselle Harriet had rather be
Mrs. Oakly than Lady Trinket, why I wish her joy.
Mr. Russet, I wish you joy of your son-in-law; Mr. Oakly,
I wish you joy of the lady, and you, madam, (*to* HARRIET)
of the gentleman; and in short, I wish you all joy of one
another, 'pon honor.   *Exit,* L.

MAJOR O. Hey! what now? (*bell rings violently*)

Enter OAKLY, R. U. E.

OAKLY. (C.) D'ye hear, Major—d'ye hear?

MAJOR O. (L. C.) Zounds! what a clatter! She'll pull
down all the bells in the house.

OAKLY. My observations since I left you have confirmed
my resolution. I see plainly that her good humour, and
her ill humour, her smiles, her tears, and her fits, are all
calculated to play upon me.

MAJOR O. Did not I always tell you so? It's the way
with them all—they will be rough and smooth, and hot
and cold, and all in a breath;—anything to get the better
of us.

OAKLY. She is in all moods at present, I promise you.
There has she been in her chamber, fuming and fretting,
and despatching a messenger to me every two minutes—
servant after servant. Now she insists on my coming to
her—now again she writes a note to entreat—then Toilet
is sent to let me know that she is ill, absolutely dying—
then, the very next minute she'll never see my face again
she'll go out of the house directly. (*bell rings*) Again!
now the storm rises!

MAJOR O. It will soon drive this way, then. Now,

brother, prove yourself a man—you have gone too far to retreat.

OAKLY. Retreat!—retreat! No, no!—I'll preserve the advantage I have gained, I am determined.

MAJOR O. Ay, ay! keep your ground—fear nothing—up with your noble heart! Good discipline makes good soldiers: stick close to my advice, and you may stand buff to a tigress——

OAKLY. Here she is, by heavens! now, brother!

MAJOR O. And now, brother!—Now or never!

Enter MRS. OAKLY, R. U. E.

MRS. O. I think, Mr. Oakly, you might have had humanity enough to have come to see how I did. You have taken your leave, I suppose, of all tenderness and affection—but I'll be calm—I'll not throw myself into a passion — you want to drive me out of your house—I see what you aim at, and will be aforehand with you—let me keep my temper! I'll send for a chair, and leave the house this instant. (*going* L. OAKLY *stops her*)

OAKLY. True, my love; I knew you would not think of dining in your chamber alone when I had company below. You shall sit at the head of the table, as you ought, to be sure, as you say, and make my friends welcome.

MRS. O. Excellent raillery! Lookye, Mr. Oakly, I see the meaning of all this affected coolness and indifference.

OAKLY. My dear, consider where you are——

MRS. O. You would be glad, I find, to get me out of your house, and have all your flirts about you.

OAKLY. Before all this company! Fie!

MRS. O. But I'll disappoint you, for I shall remain in it, to support my due authority; as for you, Major Oakly—— (*crosses to* R. C.)

MAJOR O. Hey-day! What have I done?

MRS. O. I think you might find better employment, than to create divisions between married people. (*to* OAKLY) And you, sir!——

OAKLY. (R.) Nay, but my dear!——

MRS. O. Might have more sense, as well as tenderness, than to give ear to such idle stuff.

OAKLY. Lord, lord!

MRS. O. You and your wise counsellor there, I suppose, think to carry all your points with me——

OAKLY. Was ever anything——

MRS. O. But it won't do, sir. You shall find that I will have my own way, and that I will govern my own family. (*crosses to* L.)

OAKLY. (c.) You had better learn to govern yourself, by half. Your passion makes you ridiculous. Did ever any body see so much fury and violence; affronting your best friends, breaking my peace, and disconcerting your own temper! And all for what? For nothing. 'Sdeath, madam! at these years you ought to know better.

MRS. O. (L.) At these years! Very fine! Am I to be talked to in this manner?

OAKLY. Talked to! Why not? You have talked to me long enough,—almost talked me to death,—and I have taken it all, in hopes of making you quiet; but all in vain. Patience, I find, is all thrown away upon you; and henceforward, come what may, I am resolved to be master f my own house.

MRS. O. So, so! Master, indeed! Yes, sir; and you'll take care to have mistresses enough too, I warrant you!

OAKLY. Perhaps I may; but they shall be quiet ones, I can assure you.

MRS. O. Indeed! And do you think I am such a tame fool as to sit quietly and bear all this? You shall find that I have a spirit—— (*crosses to* R.)

OAKLY. (c.) Of the devil.

MRS. O. (R.) Intolerable! you shall find then that I will exert that spirit. I am sure I have need of it. As soon as the house is once cleared again, I'll shut my doors against all company. You shan't see a single soul for this month.

OAKLY. 'Sdeath, madam, but I will! I'll keep open house for a year. I'll send cards to the whole town—Mr. Oakly's rout! All the world will come, and I'll go among the world too; I'll be mewed up no longer.

MRS. O. Provoking insolence! This is not to be endured —Lookye, Mr. Oakly——

OAKLY. And lookye, Mrs. Oakly, I will have my own way.

MRS. O. Nay, then, let me tell you, sir—

OAKLY. And let me tell you, madam, I will not be crossed—I won't be made a fool.

MRS. O. Why, you won't let me speak.

OAKLY. Because you don't speak as you ought. Madam, madam! you shan't look, nor walk, nor talk, nor think, but as I please!

MRS. O. That it should ever come to this!—To be contradicted—(*sobbing*)—insulted—abused—hated, it is too much—my heart will burst with—oh—oh!—(*falls into a fit in chair*, c.—HARRIET, CHARLES, *&c. run to her assistance*)

OAKLY. (c. *interposing*) Let her alone.

HAR. (*up* L. c.) Sir, Mrs. Oakly——

CHARLES. (*up* L. c.) For heaven's sake, sir, she will be——

OAKLY. Let her alone—let her alone.

HAR. Pray, my dear sir, let us assist her. She may——

OAKLY. I don't care—Let her alone, I say.

MRS. O. (*who has been screaming, rises suddenly*) O, you monster!—you villain!—you base man!—Would you let me die for want of help?—would you——

OAKLY. Bless me! madam, your fit is very violent—take care of yourself.

MRS. O. (*crosses to* L.) Despised, ridiculed—but I'll be revenged—you shall see, sir——

OAKLY. Tol-de-rol lol-de-rol lol-de-rol-lol. (*singing*)

MRS. O. What, am I made a jest of? Exposed to all the world! If there's law or justice—— (*crosses to* R.)

OAKLY. Tol-de-rol lol-de-rol lol-de-rol-lol. (*singing*)

MRS. O. Have a care, sir; you may repent this.—Scorned and made ridiculous! No power on earth shall hinder my revenge! (*going*)

HAR. (*down* R. *interposing*) Stay, madam.

MRS. O. (R. c.) Let me go—I cannot bear this place!

HAR. Let me beseech you, madam.

MAJOR O. (L. c.) Courage, brother — you have done wonders. (*apart*)

OAKLY. (*up* c.) I think she'll have no more fits. (*apart*)

HAR. Stay, madam—pray stay but one moment.—

have been a painful witness of your uneasiness, and in great part the innocent occasion of it. Give me leave then——

Mrs. O. I did not expect, indeed, to have found you here again. But, however,——

Har. I see the agitation of your mind, and it makes me miserable. Suffer me to tell the real truth — I can explain everything to your satisfaction.

Mrs. O. May be so—I cannot argue with you.

Charles. Pray, madam, hear her, for my sake, for your own, dear madam!

Mrs. O. Well, well—proceed.

Har. I understand, madam, that your first alarm was occasioned by a letter from my father to your nephew.

Russet. (l.) I was in a swinging passion, to be sure, madam! The letter was not over civil, I believe. But it's all over now, and so——

Mrs. O. You was here yesterday, sir?

Russet. Yes, I came after Harriet. I thought I should find my young madam with my young sir, here.

Mrs. O. With Charles, did you say, sir?

Russet. Ay, with Charles, madam. The young rogue has been fond of her a long time, and she of him, it seems. I ask pardon, madam, for the disturbance I made in your house.

Mrs. O. How have I been mistaken! (aside) But did not I overhear you and Mr. Oakly? (to Harriet)

Har. Dear madam, you had but a partial hearing of our conversation. It related entirely to this gentleman.

Charles. To put it beyond doubt, madam, Mr. Russet and my guardian have consented to our marriage, and we are in hopes that you will not withhold your approbation.

Mrs. O. I have no further doubt—I see you are innocent, and it was cruel to suspect you. You have taken a load of anguish off my mind; and yet your kind interposition comes too late: Mr. Oakly's love for me is entirely destroyed. (weeping)

Oakly. I must go to her. (apart)

Major O. Not yet—not yet! (apart)

Har. Do not disturb yourself with such apprehensions; am sure Mr. Oakly loves you most affectionately.

OAKLY. I can hold no longer. (*going to her*) My affection for you, madam, is as warm as ever. My constrained behaviour has cut me to the soul—for it was all constrained—and it was with the utmost difficulty that I was able to support it.

MRS. O. O, Mr. Oakly, what low arts has my jealousy induced me to practise! I see my folly, and fear that you can never forgive me.

OAKLY. Forgive you?—this change transports me! Brother—Mr. Russet—Charles—Harriet—give me joy; I am the happiest man in the world!

MAJOR O. Joy, much joy to you both!—though, by-the-bye, you are not a little obliged to me for it. Did not I tell you I would cure all the disorders in your family? I beg pardon, sister, for taking the liberty to prescribe for you. My medicines have been somewhat rough, I believe, but they have had an admirable effect, and so don't be angry with your physician.

MRS. O. I am indeed obliged to you, and I feel——

OAKLY. Nay, my dear, no more of this. All that's past must be utterly forgotten.

MRS. O. I have not merited this kindness, but it shall hereafter be my study to deserve it. Away with all idle jealousies! And since my suspicions have hitherto been groundless, I am resolved for the future never to suspect at all

CHARLES.   HARRIET.   MRS. O.   OAKLY.   MAJOR O.   RUSSET.

R.   L.

Curtain.

www.ingramcontent.com/pod-product-compliance
Lightning Source LLC
Chambersburg PA
CBHW021246260626
47172CB00002B/853